JAKE MADDOX
GRAPHIC NOVELS

DANCE TEAM DOUBLE TROUBLE

STONE ARCH BOOKS
a capstone imprint

JAKE MADDOX
GRAPHIC NOVELS

are published by Stone Arch Books,
an imprint of Capstone.
1710 Roe Crest Drive
North Mankato, Minnesota 56003
www.capstonepub.com

Library of Congress Cataloging-in-Publication Data
is available on the Library of Congress website.

ISBN: 978-1-4965-9713-7 (hardcover)
ISBN: 978-1-4965-9923-0 (paperback)
ISBN: 978-1-4965-9758-8 (eBook PDF)

Summary: When twins Lydia and Marco are
approached to be on their dance studio's jazz team,
Lydia is thrilled. She and Marco both love to dance
and used to have fun dancing together as kids. But
lately it seems their relationship has grown more
distant. Lydia can't wait to dance with her brother
again, but Marco is worried. He's used to hip-hop
and will be the only boy on the team. And when
bullies start mocking Marco for doing "girl dances"
it could spell trouble for the whole team.

Designer: Cynthia Della-Rovere
Production: Tori Abraham

Printed in the United States of America.
PA117

DANCE TEAM DOUBLE TROUBLE

TEXT BY
KATIE SCHENKEL

ART BY
MEL JOY SAN JUAN

COLOR BY
ROHVEL YUMUL

LETTERING BY
JAYMES REED

COVER ART BY
BERENICE MUNIZ

STARTING LINEUP

LYDIA

MARCO

MOM

MAMI

BROOKE

COACH TIA

JAMIE

SHAWN

Nothing makes me happier than spending time at Brownsville Dance Academy.

Good, Lydia!

I've been dancing since I could walk. Four years ago I started taking ballet here. Now I'm in jazz classes too.

Dancing is hard work, but it makes me so happy. I feel free when I'm in the studio.

Good job, girls. See you on Thursday.

Hey, Marco.

Hey, sis.

Marco is my twin brother.

He's been dancing as long as I have.

He started with me in ballet but eventually switched to hip-hop.

The hip-hop classes have more boys. Marco seems to like that better.

Marco and I have always been close. Our moms used to say we were two peas in a pod.

When we were little, we used to dance together all the time. We were always making up our own routines.

But now that Marco is into hip-hop, we have different schedules. We barely spend any time together.

8

All right, five-minute break!

You looked good out there.

Oh, thanks.

You're the March-Garcia twins, right? I was hoping to catch you today.

I'm Coach Tía.

You coach the Academy's competitive jazz team!

Yep, the Electric Sliders.

You'll still take your regular dance classes, plus you'll have team practices. We'll be doing several weeks of training before competition starts. It'll take a lot of discipline.

Our first practice is next week. Are you interested?

This was a dream come true! Plus Marco and I would finally get to dance together again!

Uh, well we have to talk to our moms first . . .

But I definitely want to do it!

Let me know for sure by Friday. The girls will be so excited to meet you both!

What about boys? Are there any guys on the team?

Not yet. But there will be once you've joined, Marco!

Hopefully Coach Tia will let me be on the team alone.

Even if it's not as exciting without Marco.

Hey, so . . .

I've been thinking about it, and you were right.

About what?

About the team being a great opportunity. I don't want to miss out on it.

Does that mean . . .

Let's do it. It'll be fun to dance together again.

EEEEEE!

Oof!

You promise you'll have my back?

Promise. You can count on me.

19

That felt so good.

Good job, team. Get some rest. I'll see you back here tomorrow.

Having the hip-hop moves in there is a lot of fun. And honestly, dancing with all girls wasn't so bad.

Lydia! Marco! Hold up.

What's up?

We have to do our good-luck chant.

It's an end-of-practice tradition.

With every practice, we got better and better at the moves in Coach Tia's routine.

Marco and I were getting really good at the jazz layout. Our movements were totally synchronized.

Woo!

Hmmm . . .

24

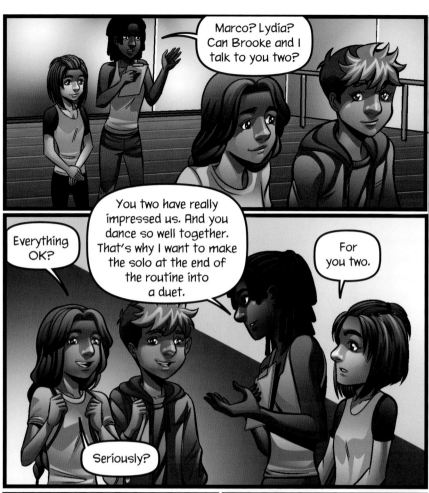

Marco? Lydia? Can Brooke and I talk to you two?

You two have really impressed us. And you dance so well together. That's why I want to make the solo at the end of the routine into a duet.

Everything OK?

For you two.

Seriously?

So? What do you say?

YES!

Practicing with Marco felt like the old days. I was just so happy to be close to him again.

But I didn't know what was about to happen. . . .

I can't believe the first competition is coming up so soon. Do you think we're ready?

You bet! We're going to blow the judges away.

I was talking to Brooke the other day. The girls were thinking—

GIRLS?

Wow, Marco. I knew you danced, but I didn't realize you did *girl* dances!

HAHA!

Nice one, Jamie!

35

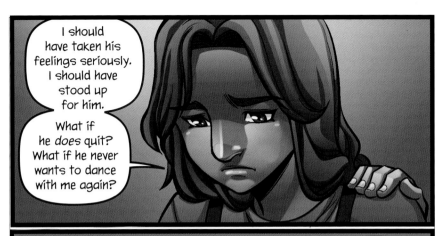

I should have taken his feelings seriously. I should have stood up for him.

What if he *does* quit? What if he never wants to dance with me again?

We can't force him to stay on the team.

Maybe you can talk to him, Lydia. It sounds like you guys need to have a conversation either way.

But, Brooke, the routine—

SIGH!

I knew Brooke was right. I needed to talk to Marco.

I'm sure Lydia didn't mean to break her promise.

It's not just that, Mami.

Those guys are right. I'm the only boy on a girly dance team. It's embarrassing.

Now hold on a second.

Do you really think dancing has to be a girl or boy thing?

I mean, yeah . . . ?

The dance team is definitely a girl thing. I told Lydia I was worried about that from the start.

Would you tell the girls in your hip-hop class that they're doing a boy thing?

That's not the same, Mom.

No, *mijito*, she's right.

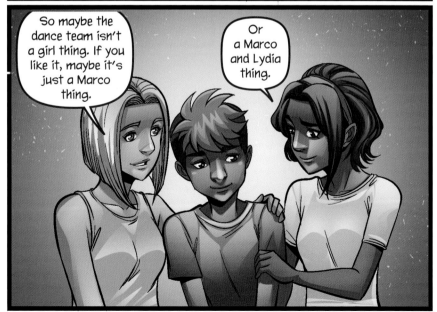

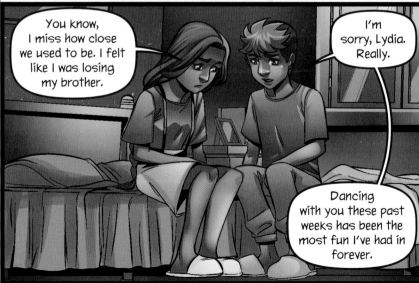

Does that mean you're staying on the team?

I'm not sure. I don't want to let anyone down. But I need to think about it.

Hey, do you want to dance with me? Not the routine. Just for fun?

I'd love that.

As Marco and I danced together, I realized something. . . .

No matter what Marco decided, we would find a way to dance with each other again. We could always come back together.

Thanks for agreeing to talk to me.

Ever since those guys started teasing me, I've felt awful. It really made me think about quitting.

Those boys sound like real jerks, Marco.

What does this mean for the team? Are you quitting or what?

Yeah, but I'm still sorry I let it get to me—and hurt our team.

Hey! Chill out.

Marco, we need to know what you've decided. If you're not going to dance with us, we have to change the routine.

Whatever you've decided is OK, Marco. I've got your back.

I thought about it, and . . .

I like dancing with you all too much to quit.

Yes!

I'm so glad, Marco. I meant what I said, though. I'll always have your back.

All right, kids. Are you ready to stretch?

Glad to have you back.

Thanks, Brooke. For the first time in weeks, I'm actually looking forward to the competition!

That weekend . . .

I can't believe we're at our first competition already.

I know. I'm just glad we're here together.

Come on, guys! We can't do our team chant without you.

And we can't perform without doing the chant.

We can do this. Let all the nerves fall away.

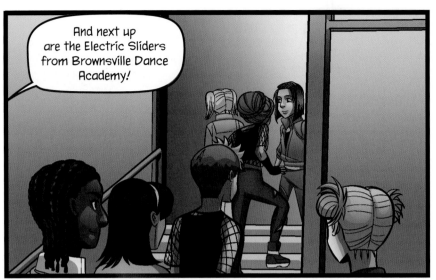

And next up are the Electric Sliders from Brownsville Dance Academy!

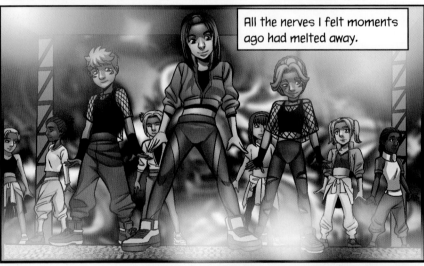

All the nerves I felt moments ago had melted away.

I had so many people rooting for me.

Including my brother. No matter what, we were a team.

One, two, three, four . . .

Chassé.

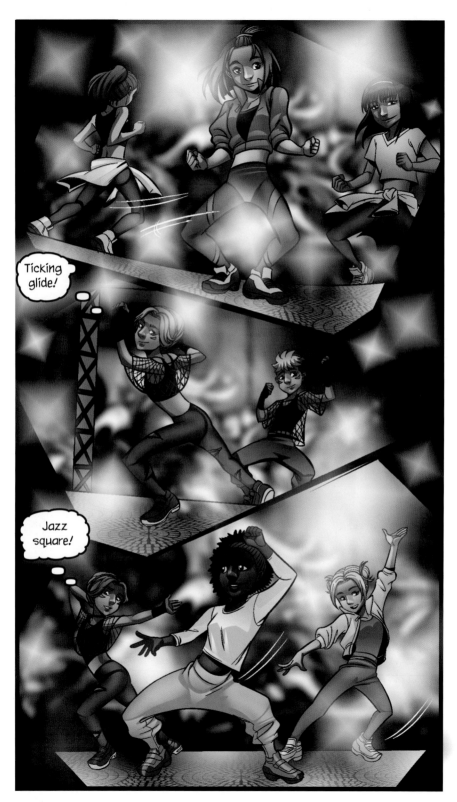

52

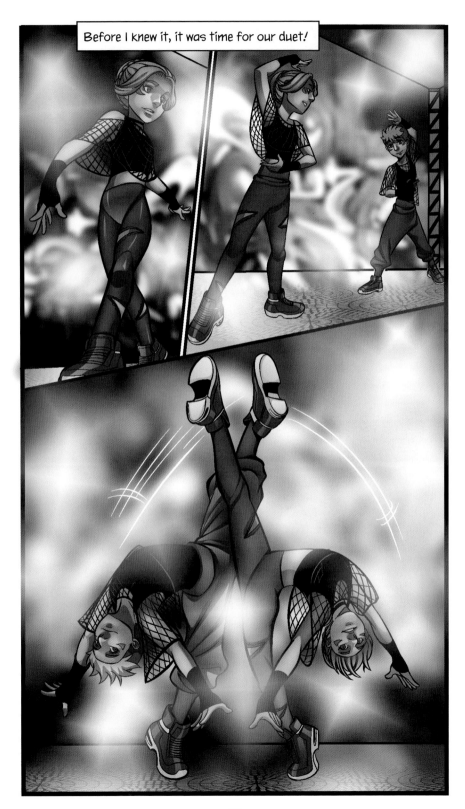

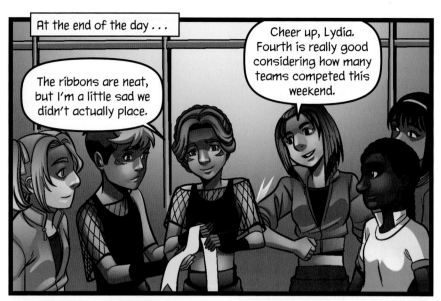

At the end of the day . . .

Cheer up, Lydia. Fourth is really good considering how many teams competed this weekend.

The ribbons are neat, but I'm a little sad we didn't actually place.

We'll do even better next time.

Plus, it's not over yet.

Huh?

And now for the special judges' awards!

CLAP! CLAP! CLAP!

The emotions you kids brought to your performance blew me away.

You clearly have a lot of fun dancing with each other.

I expect great things from your team in the future.

Thank you, sir.

CLAP! CLAP! CLAP! CLAP!

Coach Tia took us to the best pizza place in town to celebrate. . . .

I'm going to put our order in. Cheese and pepperoni OK for everyone?

Yes!

Boy, I'm starving!

Me too. Dancing really works up an appetite!

Well, well, well. Look who we have here.

VISUAL QUESTIONS

1. The art in graphic novels can tell you just as much about what's happening as the text. How do you think Marco and Lydia each feel when Coach Tia invites them to be on the jazz team? How are their reactions alike or different? What clues help you figure it out?

2. Marco is upset with Lydia for not standing up for him when he's being bullied. But Lydia doesn't realize that Marco is upset. How does this difference in opinions build throughout the story? Look back through the art and choose 2–3 panels that help foreshadow their disagreement.

3. Marco loves to dance, but threatens to quit the team. What do his body language and facial expression in this panel tell you about how he's feeling?

4. The Electric Sliders win a special award for team passion. Look at their performance in the competition and choose a panel that you think best shows this skill. What about the art makes you think they deserve that award?

MORE ABOUT DANCE

There are many different types of dance, but joining the jazz team is what brings Lydia and Marco back together. Want to learn more about this style of dance? Here are some of the basic terms and moves.

ball change—a changing of weight between the balls of the feet

chaîné—a series of short, usually fast turns a dancer uses to move across the stage

chassé—a kind of gallop where one foot chasses the other; this is a basic ballet step and a traveling step

drop—when a dancer performs a fall from a position he or she is holding; this is used in more modern dance routines

extension—when an arm or leg is extended outward and held there for a specific amount of time

fan kick—a kick where the body stays in place, but one leg starts inward and kicks all the way around to its start position

jazz square—a smooth, four-step movement that has a dancer stepping out on the right leg, back with the left, crossing over the right leg and then stepping forward with the left to create a full square shape

jazz walk—a type of walk where the body is in plié and the feet drag slightly across the floor; this is often used for traveling across the stage

knee turn—a basic chaîné turn done on one or both knees

layout—when a dancer is leaned back in a dramatic arch with one leg kicked up in the air, head back, and arms extended, almost touching the floor

pivot step—a dancer steps one foot in front of the other, then pivots around to his or her start position

release—following a pose, a dancer "releases" into a more-relaxed form

stag leap—a very high jump done while performing splits in the air at the same time; one leg is bent in the air so the foot is tucked under the knee

GLOSSARY

competition (kahm-puh-TI-shuhn)—a contest between two or more people

discipline (DIS-uh-plin)—self-control and the ability to follow the rules

dress rehearsal (dres ri-HURSS-uhl)—the final practice of a performance that is done with all the costumes, scenery, etc., that will be used in the first real performance before an audience

duet (doo-ET)—two people performing together

opportunity (op-er-TOO-ni-tee)—a chance for greater success

recital (ri-SIGH-tuhl)—a dance or musical performance

rehearsal (ri-HURSS-uhl)—a practice performance

routine (roo-TEEN)—a series of things that are repeated as part of a performance

solo (SOH-loh)—a performance done by one person

synchronized (SING-kruh-nized)—when two or more people perform the same movements at the same time

tradition (truh-DISH-uhn)—a group of people's longtime ways of doing things